Young Learner's

Jungle Tales

The Moving Tail

The Hungry Sloth

The Moving Tail

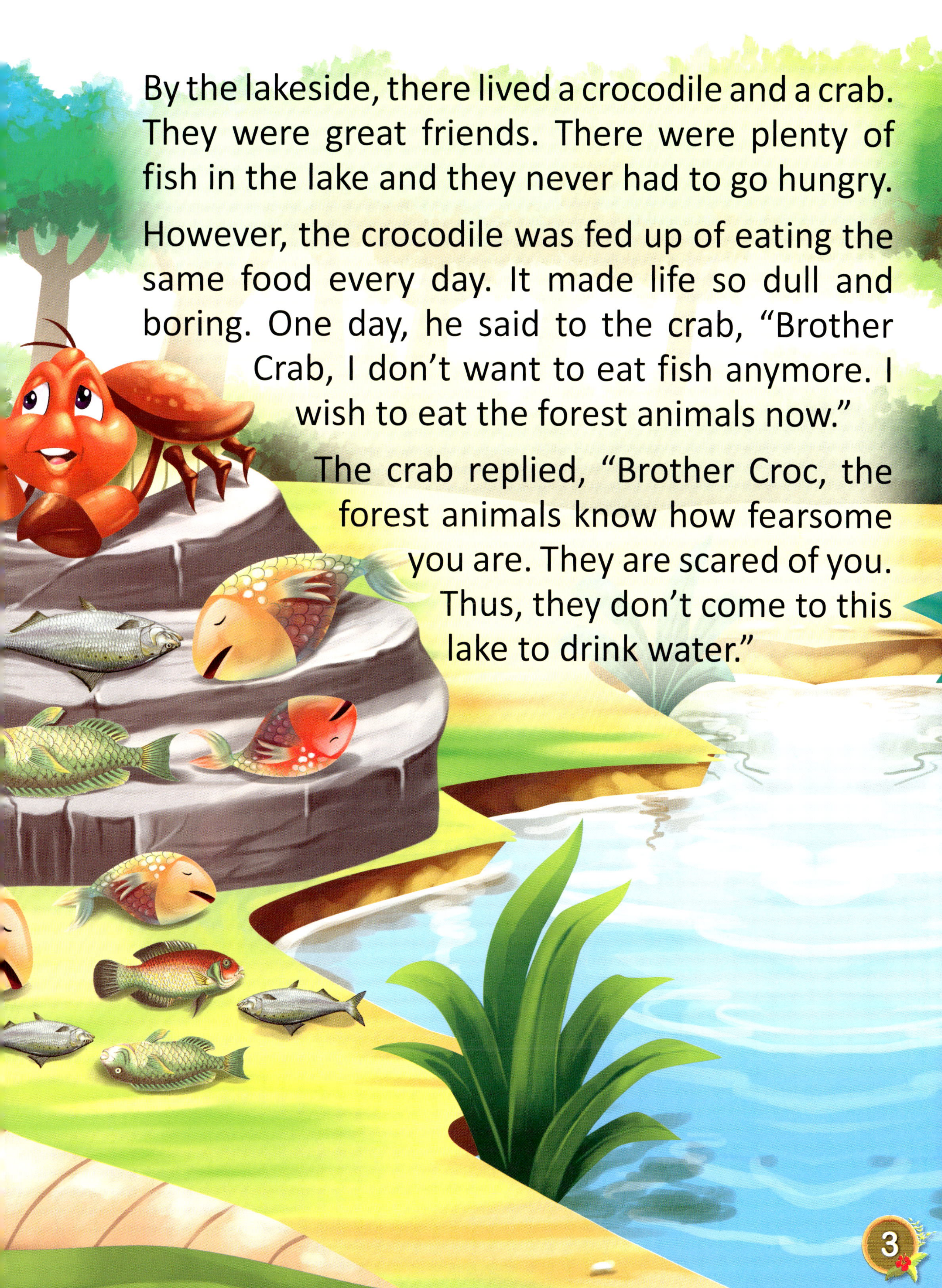

By the lakeside, there lived a crocodile and a crab. They were great friends. There were plenty of fish in the lake and they never had to go hungry.

However, the crocodile was fed up of eating the same food every day. It made life so dull and boring. One day, he said to the crab, "Brother Crab, I don't want to eat fish anymore. I wish to eat the forest animals now."

The crab replied, "Brother Croc, the forest animals know how fearsome you are. They are scared of you. Thus, they don't come to this lake to drink water."

"Yes, I know," replied the crocodile sadly. The crab suggested, "What if we spread the word that you are dead? That way the animals would start coming to the lake again. You can pretend to lie dead, and when they are drinking water you can pounce on them from behind."

"Excellent idea, Brother Crab!" exclaimed the crocodile, "Now go and tell everyone that I am dead. I will wait here for you and the forest animals."

The crab went into the forest and began crying loudly. He called out to the monkey sitting on a tree and told him that his dear friend, crocodile, was lying dead by the lakeside. The excited monkey went around the forest telling the animals about the dead crocodile.

The animals were so happy for now they would not have to go to the faraway lake to drink water. But, the fox had his doubts. He decided to go to the lakeside and find out the truth. At the lakeside, he saw the crocodile lying still in the water and the crab sitting on a rock.

Seeing the fox, the crab called out, "Brother Fox! Now that the crocodile is dead you can safely drink water from the lake."

"I am not thirsty, old crab. Are you sure the crocodile is really dead? The tails of dead crocodiles always move. This crocodile's tail is not moving at all!" said the fox, pointing at the crocodile's tail.

Hearing this, the foolish crocodile started moving his tail. The fox laughed out loud, “I knew you were lying. The crocodile is not dead. It was a trap you laid to eat the forest animals.” Saying so, he ran away to the forest to tell the animals about the crab’s lie. The forest animals were saved and the foolish crocodile had no choice but to eat fish from the lake!

Moral:
Never trust a cunning person.

The Hungry Sloth

Deep in the rainforest, there lived a lazy sloth. He slept all day long. Rain or shine, he would just sleep. One hot day, he slept from morning until late evening. When he woke up, he felt very hungry. He plucked a few leaves and chewed on them, but they tasted very bitter. So, he spit them out.

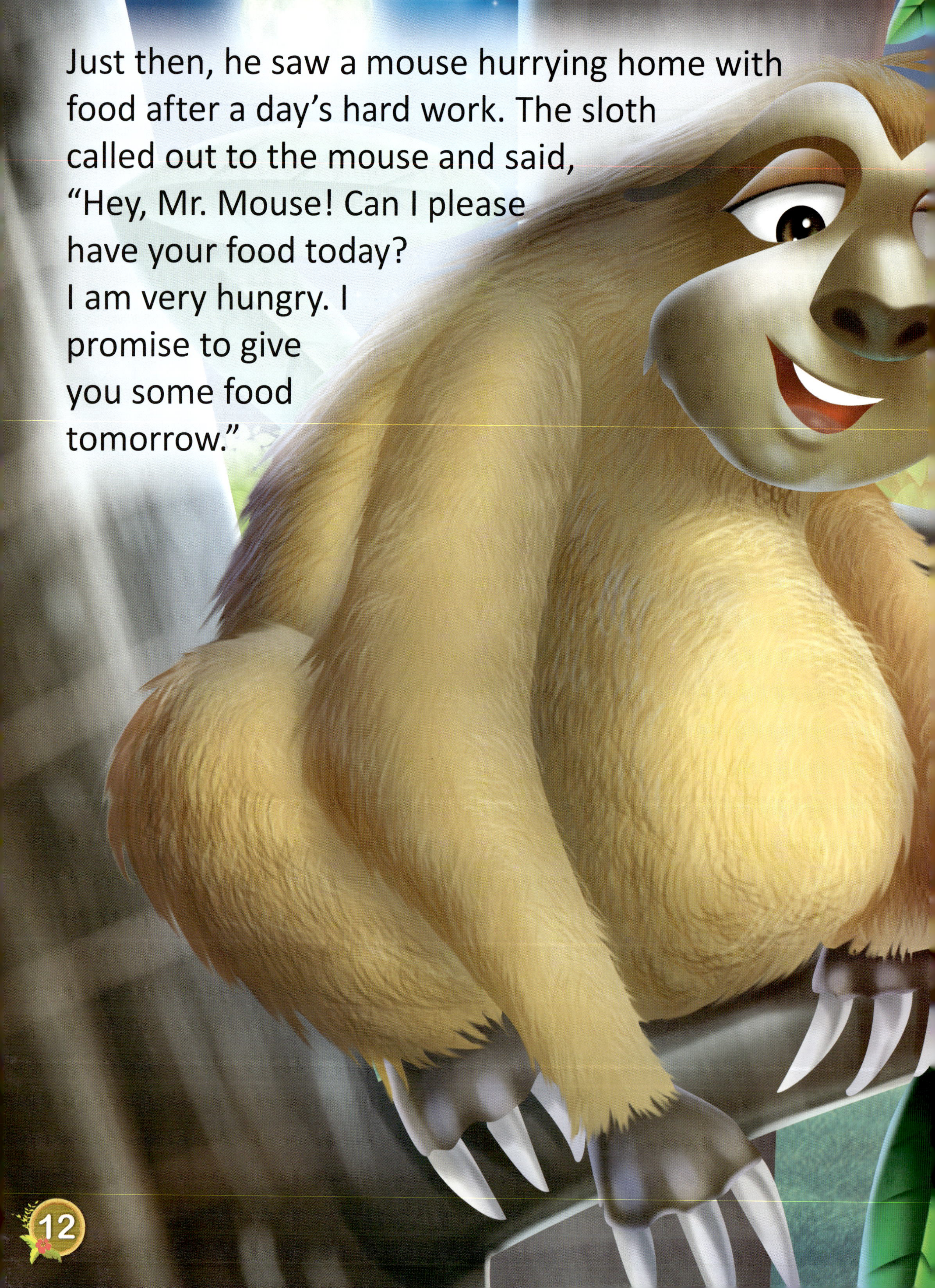

Just then, he saw a mouse hurrying home with food after a day's hard work. The sloth called out to the mouse and said, "Hey, Mr. Mouse! Can I please have your food today? I am very hungry. I promise to give you some food tomorrow."

The kind mouse smiled, "Okay, Mr. Sloth! You can have my food but remember to keep your promise." The sloth further added, "And oh! I am not too well today. Would you mind coming up and giving me the food?" The lazy sloth did not even want to climb down the tree to get the food!

The mouse happily went up the tree, gave the basket of food to the sloth, who greedily gobbled up it all.

After a while, he was hungry again. He looked around and saw a toucan flying by. As before, the sloth asked the toucan for food saying that he was unwell. He promised to give some food to the toucan the next day.

The toucan took pity on the sloth. He said, “Okay, Mr. Sloth! You can have my food but remember to keep your promise. Now, I will quickly go and get some more food for my children.”

Saying so, he dropped his load of food in front of the sloth and flew away. The sloth ate the food quickly and began to hum happily.

As night fell, the sloth was hungry again. He was hoping to find some more food when he saw a jaguar. He called out to the jaguar and said, "Mr. Jaguar, can I please have your food? I am very hungry and sick. I will give you some food tomorrow, I promise." The jaguar was not kind. In fact, he was himself very hungry. He climbed up the tree and ate up the sloth. And that was the end of the lazy sloth.

Moral:
Laziness can get you into deep trouble.